Seawall

Story by Goldie Alexander
Illustrations by Paul Könye

Rigby PM
part of the Rigby PM Collection

U.S. Edition © 2001
Harcourt Achieve Inc.
10801 N. MoPac Expressway
Building #3
Austin, TX 78759
www.harcourtachieve.com

Text © 2001 Thomson Learning Australia
Illustrations © 2001 Thomson Learning Australia
Originally published in Australia by Thomson Learning Australia

10 9 8 7
09

Seawall
  ISBN 0 7635 7787 1

Printed in China by 1010 Printing International Ltd.

Contents

Chapter 1
Market Day

It was a Tuesday in the year 2165. Dana's mother was getting ready to transport their vegetable crop to the District Market. Dana usually went with her in their hover, but this time she wanted to stay home.

"Can't I stay here on my own?" she asked.

Her mother looked doubtful. "I won't be back until tomorrow morning. What if something goes wrong?"

"Then I'll call you on this." Dana tapped the viewcom strapped to her wrist. "Please, Mom, please."

Her mother turned and looked out the window to a sky heavy with storm clouds. It was raining again. After what seemed like a long time, she sighed. "Well, I suppose so… but only if you keep Silas with you all the time, wherever you go."

Hearing his name, the old dog struggled to his feet.

"No, Mom, no," Dana cried. "He's too old. He'll only be a pest."

Mom's lips tightened. "One day you'll be old yourself."

Dana knew better than to argue. Before her mother could change her mind, Dana turned on the waterproofing controls on her coverall and dashed out the door onto the hover landing.

Her mother's voice followed her outside. "If you have any trouble, call the Bennetts." Their closest neighbors, the Bennetts, lived five miles away.

"Okay, okay," Dana yelled. "See you when you get back."

The house stood on concrete poles, high above the treeless and swampy land. Dana made her way down to the muddy paddocks below. Silas followed. After a few minutes, she turned and waved. She half expected her mother to call her back with some last-minute instructions, but to her surprise and relief, her mother merely waved. Then Dana watched as the hover rose into the sky and disappeared behind the clouds.

The old dog padded slowly after Dana. After about five minutes, he collapsed onto his haunches.

"Come on Silas, come on," cried Dana.

Silas rose slowly and whined. Dana picked up a stick and threw it. "Fetch the stick, Silas. Good dog, fetch!"

Silas whimpered and sat down again.

"Oh, go home, you silly old dog. Go home," Dana yelled impatiently. Then she turned and headed off at a run for the seawall and the water.

Chapter 2
The Chores

In 2159, there had been a giant flood, claiming a large area of excellent farm land where Dana's family lived. That was the year Dana turned six, and the year her father died. Life hadn't been easy since then. Vacations were rare events, and the daily chores seemed as endless as the dreary rain.

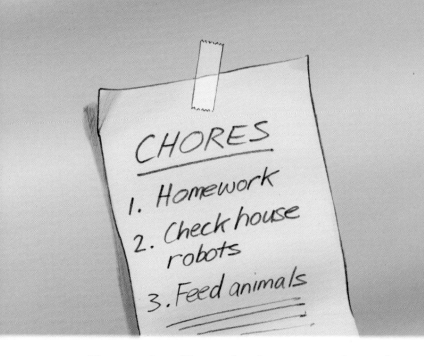

CHORES
1. Homework
2. Check house robots
3. Feed animals

Every day Dana had to complete the homework her computer sent her. Then she had to check the house robots. Her other major job was caring for the animals. Dana liked the ducks, but she didn't like the way the chickens pecked each other, or the way the two goats nipped her fingers.

Finally, and most importantly, she had to check the heat and water controls for the indoor greenhouse where they grew their crop of tomatoes, beans, and broccoli.

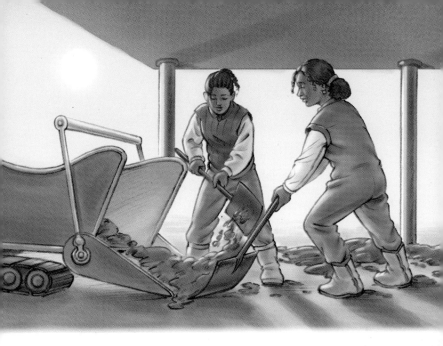

During the brief dry periods, Dana helped clear the mud from under the house.

Sometimes her mother complained of having too much to do. Dana would remind her that most of their neighbors had gone to live in safe inland cities such as Skipton and Oodna. She always knew, though, what her mother's reply would be.

"Your father drowned trying to save this land from the sea. There's no way that the sea will beat me, too."

Chapter 3

The Wall

Dana's run brought her to the base of the great seawall. This wall was the most important thing in their lives.

"If we neglect that wall," her mother said, "the sea will take the rest of this land."

Dana's mother and the Bennetts looked after the seawall for the District Elders. In return, the Elders had helped Dana's mother build an indoor greenhouse. Now they could still grow vegetables for the District Market, even though the land around the house could no longer be farmed.

The wall was huge. Built from concrete and rocks, it rose twenty yards into the air. It was five yards wide at the base, narrowing to barely a foot at the top. Each time Dana saw it, it looked different. Sometimes it rose into the sky, strong and fierce like a mountain. Other times it seemed like a gentle hill flowing up from the plains.

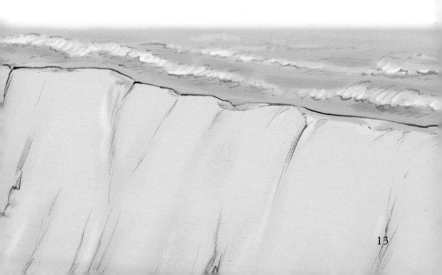

Dana started to climb up the wall. After years of practice, she could reach the top in just under six minutes. She knew where to find the tiny ledges for her feet. She knew to watch for crumbling stones and flatten herself against the wind.

The effort was worth it. From a ledge at the wall's highest point, she could see far out to sea. To the adults, the sea was a constant threat, but Dana loved it. She loved the reckless way the breakers dashed themselves against the wall. She loved the way they formed white crests like yacht sails before falling away.

There were no birds to see, though—at least not anymore. An old book she had seen in the local museum showed photos of birds that had once lived here. "Coots, herons, snipe, magpies, geese, moorhens, gulls." She rolled their names over in her mind.

Dana looked down at the raging surf. Fifteen yards below, the waves swirled and twirled. When the sea was like this, it reminded her of that great gray monster, the killer shark. Sometimes she dreamed that the shark was waiting to attack. Then she would wake in a cold sweat.

She made her way carefully along the narrow wall. On one side was the menacing, sucking sea; on the other, the steamy swamplands. It was dangerous on the rim, but Dana loved feeling like she was at the top of the world. She looked to the land below and saw a reddish streak far off in the distance. "Go home, Silas," she yelled. "Go home, you silly old dog."

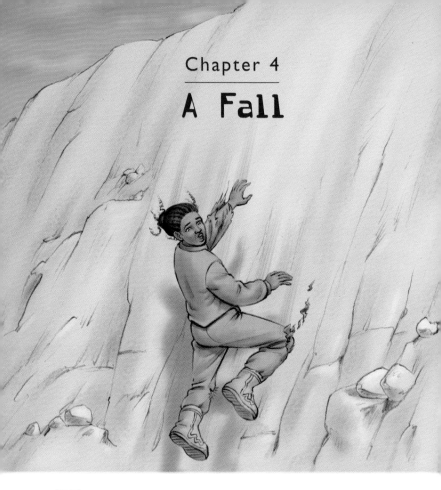

Chapter 4

A Fall

Feeling guilty about Silas, Dana continued along the wall. The surface was wet and slippery and the wind tore at her. Suddenly, she stumbled. Unable to keep her balance, she threw her weight to the land side of the wall and slid down, down, until a cluster of rocks and a ledge stopped her fall.

She sat still for a moment, eyes closed and breathing deeply. Then she sat up and looked around. She had slid almost to the base of the wall. Slowly she felt herself all over—no broken bones. But her coverall was torn, her knees were scraped, and her hands were scratched and bloody.

And her feet were wet.

Puzzled, she looked down. Her feet had landed heavily in an opening among the rocks. She clambered out and bent down for a closer look. There was a pool of muddy water, which grew larger as she watched. Where was the water coming from? She put her hand in the pool and felt around. Her exploring fingers quickly found a small hole, a crack between the rocks and concrete. She placed her hand in the hole and felt a rush of cold water on her fingers.

Quickly she pulled her hand out. The pool of water grew.

Her heart started a painful *thump, thump*. Water behind the rocks just there could mean only one thing—a break in the wall. Very shortly, this break would widen. Then the all-powerful sea would come through, and the valley would drown. There would be nothing to stop it.

She plunged her hand back into the pool immediately and plugged up the hole.

It took Dana a long moment to remember that she should contact the Bennetts. She glanced down at her free wrist, where she wore her viewcom. Her wrist was bare. The viewcom had been ripped off in the fall.

Still keeping her hand in the hole, she carefully looked around. There was no sign of the viewcom—only bare rock, swampy grass, and bulrushes. She didn't dare go for help. If she left the hole unplugged, the water would flood through.

Then Dana remembered Silas. Without thinking, she removed her hand to whistle for him. The pool grew bigger. Hastily she replugged the hole with her hand and searched for a glimpse of Silas.

But she could see nothing. For once, Silas had obeyed her and gone home. There was only the wind sifting through the bulrushes, and the sea crashing against the seawall.

Dana groaned. Why had she sent the dog away? Silas would have raised an alarm. How could she have been so stupid? Now all she could do was wait for someone to realize that she was missing and come looking for her.

But no one came.

A few clouds parted to reveal a washed-out sky. And the great, gray sea on the other side of the wall sucked and tugged.

Chapter 5

Dana and the Sea

For the first hour, Dana felt fine. Then her hand went numb and she began to feel that the sea would win. The sea had Dana in its grasp, and like a well-fed cat playing with a mouse, it teased her. It nibbled here, it nibbled there. Gradually, her arm also began to lose all feeling. Then her shoulder... She longed to move, but she knew she couldn't risk making the hole wider.

Soon after noon, the clouds disappeared and the sun hung overhead like a giant lamp. The swamp steamed gently. Swamp flies appeared. Dana used her free hand to swat them away. The insects returned in even bigger numbers.

Sunburned and covered in bites, Dana began to lose track of time. The insects vanished and the sun sank. She was hungry and frightened and no one knew where she was. She longed for the comfort of old Silas.

Finally, she slept—and the dreams began. She dreamed that she was back home. She stood in front of Mom, who stared right through her. Dana called to her, shouted into her face. Still Mom couldn't see her.

Then Dana was back on the wall, sliding from one dream into another. A terrible sea serpent twisted its coils around her. The serpent had lidless eyes, a forked tongue, and widening jaws. Then the serpent changed into a great gray shark. Dana knew that pointy shape and that evil, slippery skin. The shark swam close enough for her to smell its briny breath and feel its rough skin.

Dana woke. Something was licking her face. Terrified, she started up—and was almost overwhelmed by a welcome doggy smell. Silas was barking wildly—Silas was keeping the shark at bay.

"Oh, Silas," she cried, overjoyed, reaching for the dog's shaggy neck.

Her mother's face appeared. Someone shouted, "We'll need sandbags, spades…"

Before she could explain, the world spun and toppled. Then everything turned black.

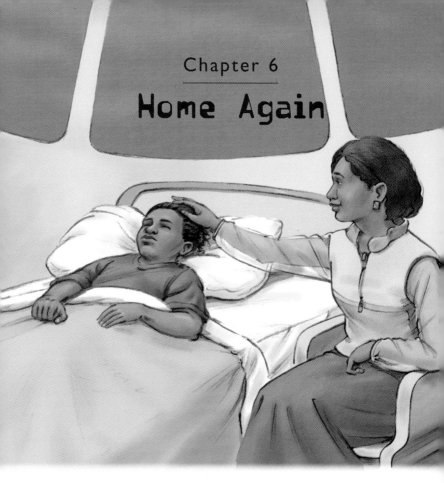

Chapter 6
Home Again

Dana's eyelids fluttered open. She was back in her own bed. Mom was beside her. For some reason, Mom kept slipping in and out of focus.

Dana's mouth was too dry to speak. "W–w–what happened?" she finally managed to ask.

Her mother stroked her forehead gently. "I came home this morning to find Silas outside, barking madly, and no sign of you. It was clear that you hadn't been home all night, and the Bennetts hadn't heard from you. But I knew Silas would be able to tell us where you were—and he did. He led us to the seawall. There you were, keeping the sea back, all on your own."

"Did I stop it from coming through?"

She nodded gravely. "You certainly did. You were very brave."

Hearing a muffled bark, Dana stretched out her hand. A raspy tongue licked it.

"I couldn't have managed it without Silas," she said slowly. "You would never have found me, and the sea would have come through eventually. The land would have been lost."

"Shhh, now," said her mother. "Time to rest."

Dana bent over Silas. "I'm sorry I was mean to you, Silas," she whispered into a shaggy ear. "From now on, we go everywhere together. We're a team."

The old dog thumped his tail enthusiastically.